W9-BZS-981

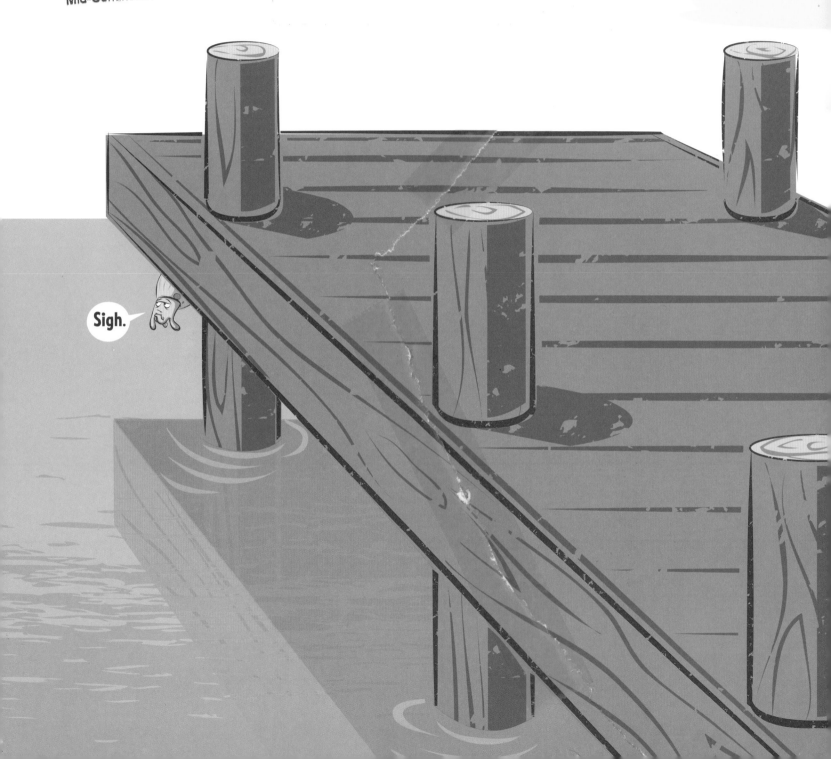

Sigh.

For Mom and Dad, with love and gratefulness.

Library of Congress Cataloging-in-Publication Data • Fenske, Jonathan, author.
Barnacle is bored / by Jonathan Fenske.—First edition. • pages cm
Summary: Barnacle is bored by the monotony of the tides, and envies the fish
who swim freely—until an eel comes along. • ISBN 978-0-545-86504-3 (paper over board)
1. Barnacles—Juvenile fiction. 2. Fishes—Juvenile fiction. 3. Boredom—Juvenile fiction.
4. Envy—Juvenile fiction. [1. Barnacles—Fiction. 2. Fishes—Fiction. 3. Boredom—Fiction.] I. Title.
PZ7.F34843Bar 2016 • [E]—dc23 • 2015029064

10 9 8 7 6 5 4 3 2 1   16 17 18 19 20
Printed in Malaysia   108
First edition, May 2016
Book design by Steve Ponzo

Barnacle Is BORED

Jonathan Fenske

Scholastic Press · New York

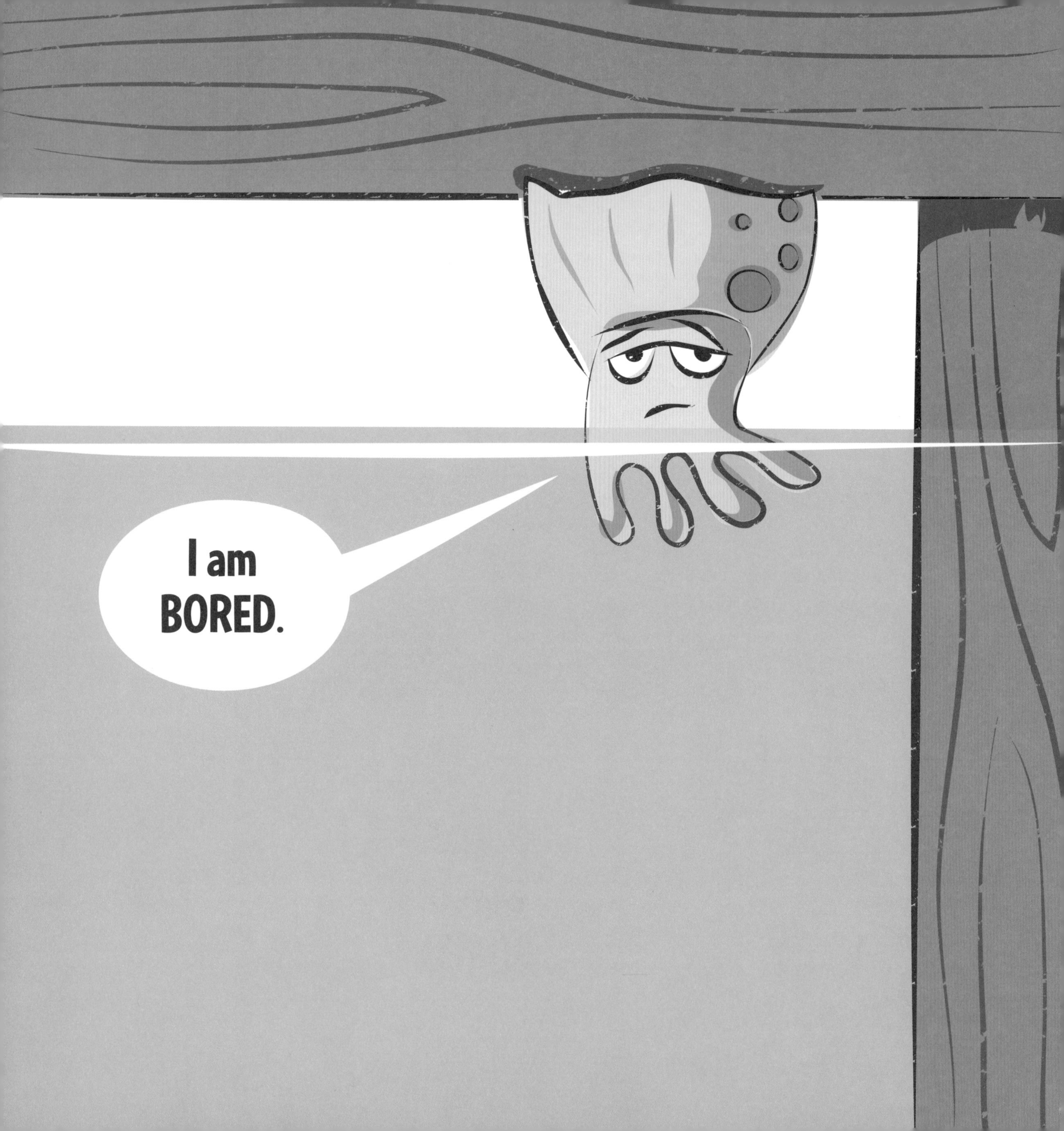
I am BORED.

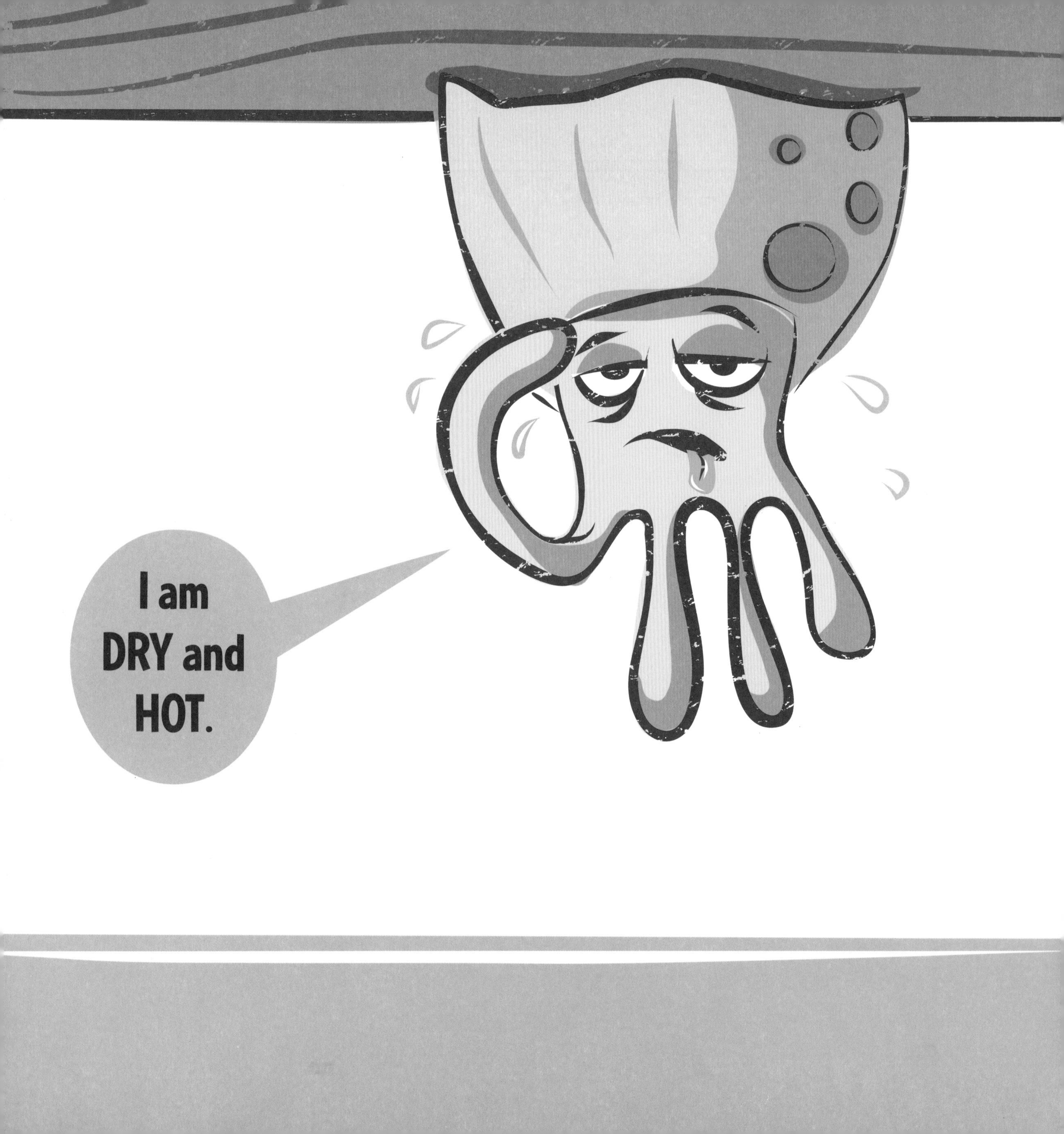
I am DRY and HOT.

Uh-oh.

I bet he ...

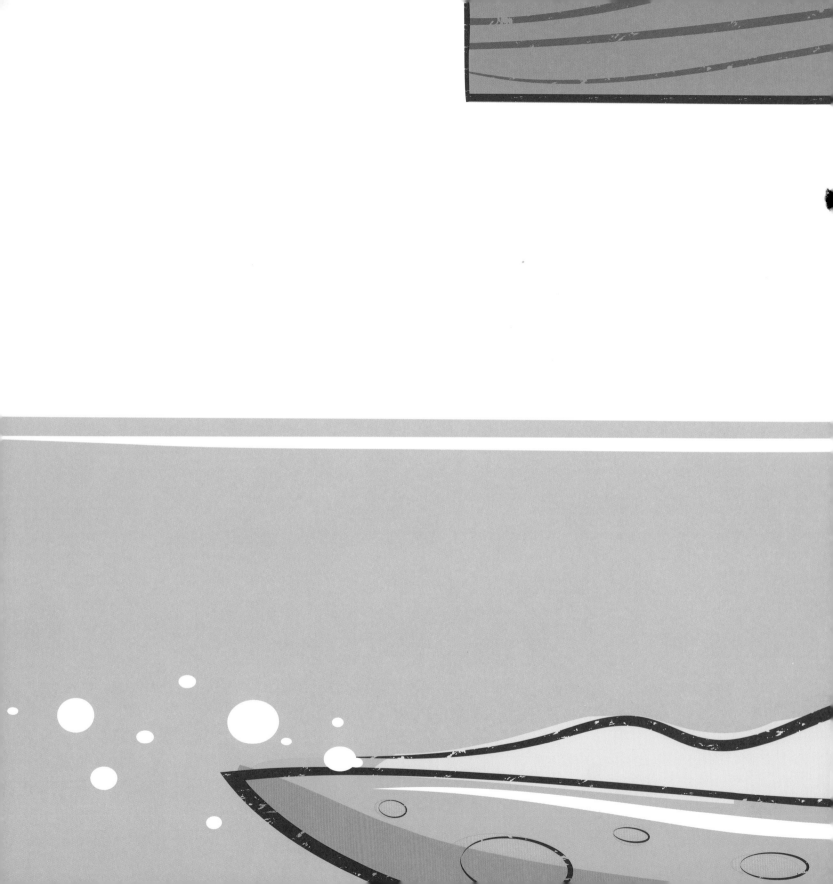

I am not bored.

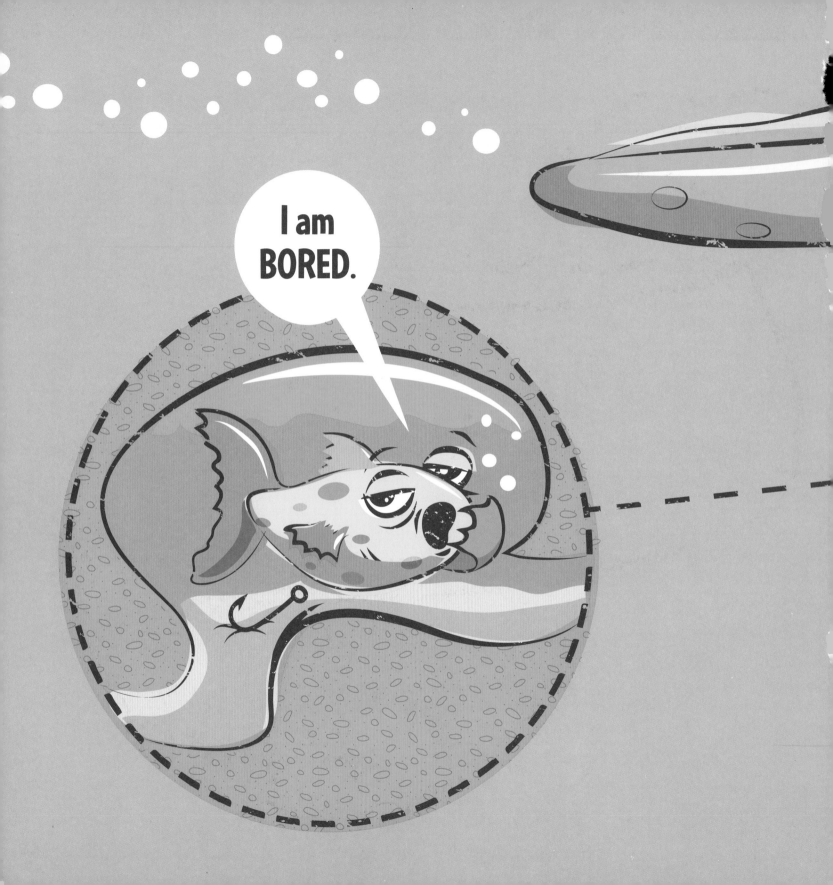